The Loon
on the
Moon

Mercury

Venus

Mars

Moon

Earth

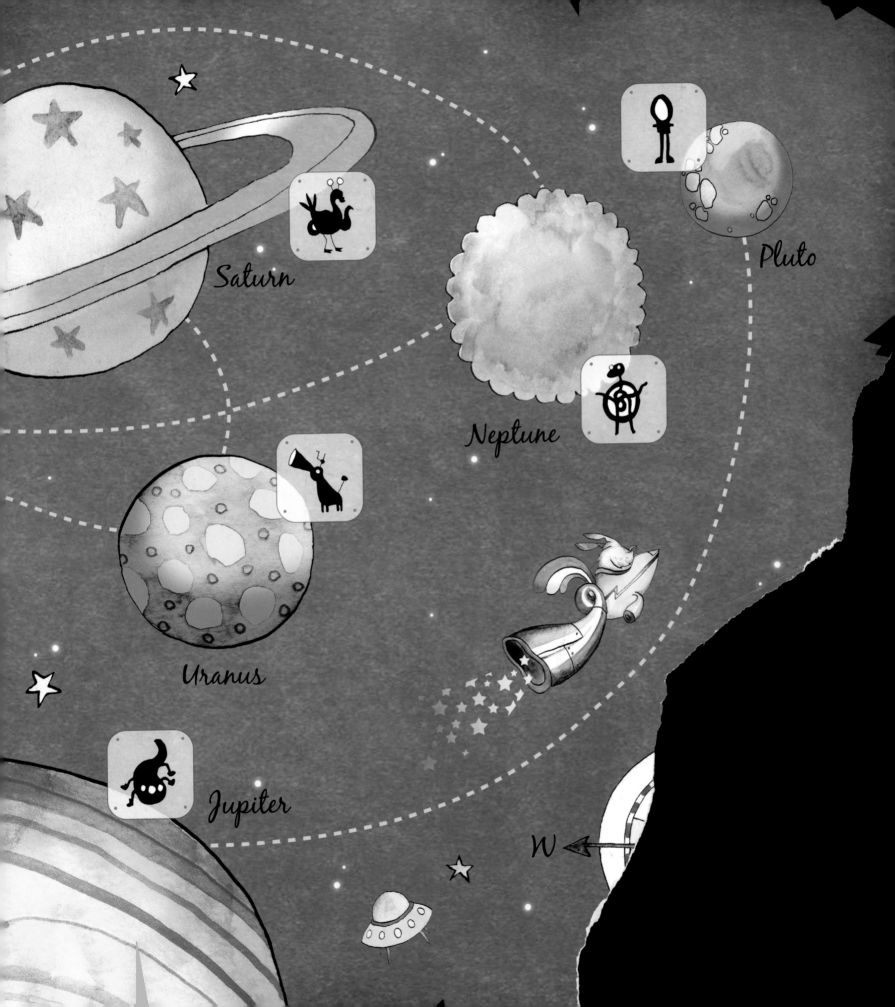

Saturn

Pluto

Neptune

Uranus

Jupiter

N

First published in 2010
by Scholastic Children's Books
Euston House, 24 Eversholt Street
London NW1 1DB
a division of Scholastic Ltd
www.scholastic.co.uk

London ~ New York ~ Toronto ~ Sydney ~
Auckland ~ Mexico City ~ New Delhi ~ Hong Kong

Text copyright © 2010 Chae Strathie
Illustrations copyright © 2010 Emily Golden

HB ISBN 978 1407108 02 5
PB ISBN 978 1407108 03 2

All rights reserved
Printed in Singapore

5 7 9 10 8 6 4

Papers used by
Scholastic Children's Books
are made from wood grown
in sustainable forests.

SCHOLASTIC

With much love
to my grandparents,
Andrew, Shelagh, Sandy
and Jessie. And to my
own little loon, Eilidh,
who makes me
laugh every day.
CS

To Grandad Jerry and
Grandad Jim for
their pens and paints.
EG

The Loon
on the
Moon

Chae Strathie

illustrated by
Emily Golden

This is the Loon
who lives on the moon.

Every night he **zooms** down to Earth in
his **Loonzoomer** to suck up all
the **dreams** that leak from children's
ears like steam from a kettle.

Then he **zooms** back up again and uses the
dream steam to power the engine...

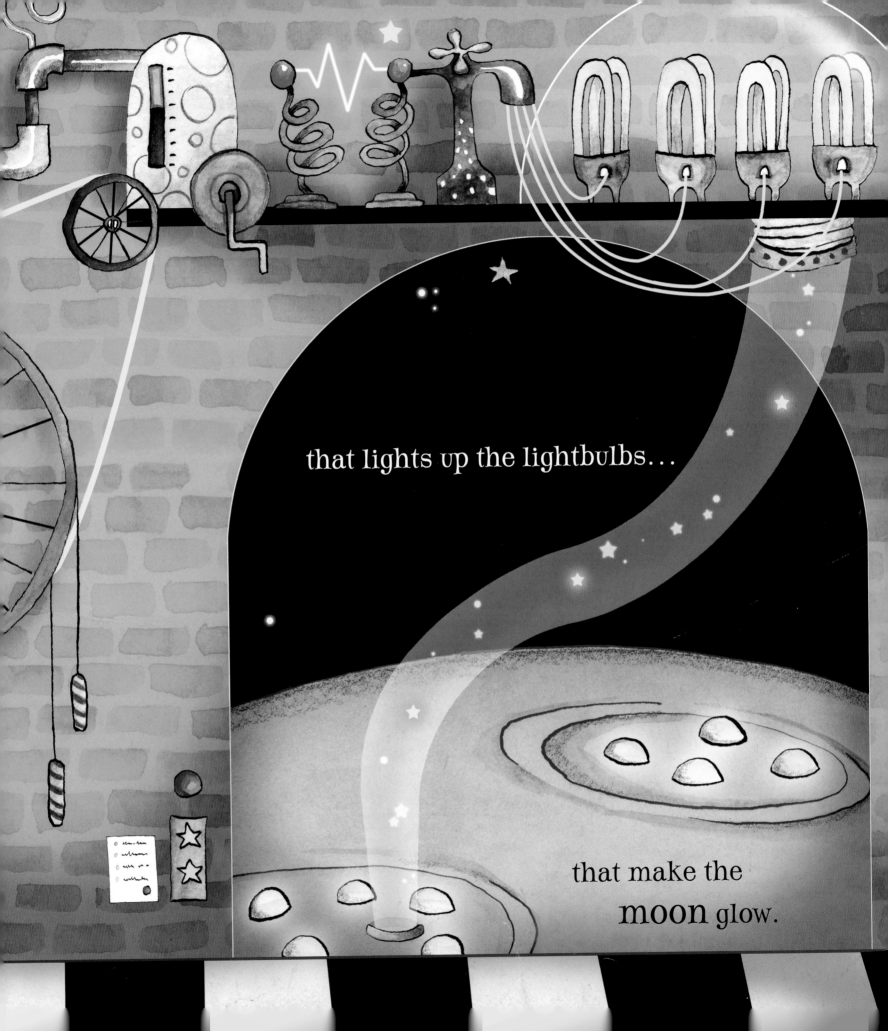

that lights up the lightbulbs...

that make the
moon glow.

But one evening, the Loon zoomed down to
find the dreams had all dried up.

"Oh dear," he said.
"Oh fizzbungle!"

(Fizzbungle is quite a naughty
word on the moon.)

"Now I'll have to get my dream steam
from somewhere else.
Perhaps the **Moptops** on
Mercury have some."

So the Loon **zoomed** with a boom to Mercury.

"Hello, Moptops.
Do you have any **dream steam**?" he asked.

The **Moptops**
stopped dancing.

"No **dream steam** here, Moon-Loon,"
they all chorused together.
"Try the **Noodles** from Neptune."

So the Loon **zoomed** with a boom to Neptune.

"Hello, **Noodles.** Do you have any **dream steam?**" he asked.

The **Noodles** were sitting
on their **Noodle** nests waiting
for their **Noodle** eggs to hatch.

"Cooo… Our **dream steam** is all
finished," they cooed.
"Try the **Vimtingles** from Venus."

So the Loon zoomed with a boom to Venus.
But the Vimtingles were far too busy telling
each other jokes and laughing until their bottoms
fell off to care about dream steam.

The **YOOHOO**ˢ from **Uranus** weren't much help either...

Nor were the **Singdings**
from Saturn…

nor the Minimoos
from Mars…

nor the **JIFFLES** from Jupiter…

nor the *Pollywollyplumpkins* from Pluto.

"Fizzbungle!"
said the Loon.

No dream steam meant
no power, which meant
no moon!

That night the Loon only
had enough power
to light up three-quarters
of the moon…

then half the next night…

then a quarter…

until finally the light
in the **moon** went
out altogether.

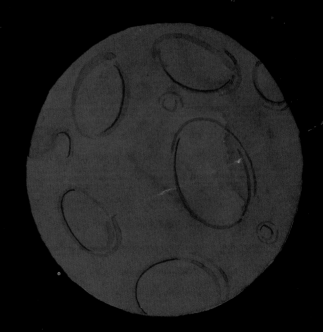

What was the Loon
going to do?

He was feeling very sad, sitting all alone
on his dark **moon**…

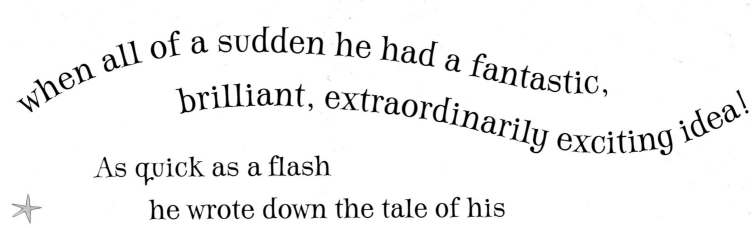

when all of a sudden he had a fantastic, brilliant, extraordinarily exciting idea!

As quick as a flash
he wrote down the tale of his
outer-space search for dream steam.

Then he wrote it again…
and again… and again…
until he had an enormous
pile of stories.

Then he zoomed with a boom
down to Earth and left a story
in every child's room.

When they heard the story
their heads were filled with

Moptops and
Noodles and
Vimtingles and JIFFLES.

And that night they
all dreamed dreams of
marvellous things…

And the Loon could light up the moon.

Mercury

Venus

Mars

Moon

Earth

Saturn

Pluto

Neptune

Uranus

Jupiter

N

W

E

S

The End